KEAN SOO
MARCH GRAND PRIX

THE RACE AT HAREWOOD

STONE ARCH BOOKS

a capstone imprint

March Grand Prix
published by Stone Arch Books,
a Capstone Imprint
1710 Roe Crest Drive
North Mankato, Minnesota 56003
www.capstonepub.com

Cataloging-in-Publication Data is available on
the Library of Congress website.

ISBN: 978-1-4342-9639-9 (library hardcover)
ISBN: 978-1-4342-9642-9 (paperback)
ISBN: 978-1-4965-0184-4 (eBook)

Summary: March Hare enters into his first
professional race at Harewood Speedway
and comes up against the defending World
Champion, Lyca the Fox, whose skills are
unrivaled. March finds help and inspiration in
the unlikeliest of places — his own family.

Printed in China by Nordica.
0415/CA21500596
042015   008843NORDF15

To Mom and Dad,

For all the times you drove me around in the backseat of the car, trying to get me to fall asleep. And for all the times I woke up as soon as we got home.

4

NOW GIRLS, BEHAVE YOURSELVES! THIS IS YOUR BROTHER'S BIG DAY! AND WHAT DO WE ALL SAY WHEN ONE OF US HAS A BIG DAY?

TODAY'S YOUR BIG DAY, IT'S TIME TO BE STRONG! WITH A HARE IN YOUR CORNER, NOTHING CAN GO WRONG!

GOOD! OH, ISN'T IT SO GLAMOROUS, HAREWOOD SHUTTING DOWN ITS CITY STREETS FOR THE BIG RACE EVERY YEAR? YOU MUST BE SO EXCITED MARCH, RACING JUST LIKE YOUR HERO, BUTTLE?

MOOOM, IT'S *TUTTLE!* ALAN TUTTLE, 3-TIME WORLD CHAMPION! SOME DAY, I'M GOING TO BREAK HIS RECORD FOR MOST CHAMPIONSHIP WINS!

WELL, HERE WE ARE.

WOW.

GOOD LUCK SWEETIE! HAVE A GREAT DAY!

MA, NOT IN FRONT OF THE OTHER DRIVERS! IT'S SO UNCOOL!

KISSY KISS ♥

OH.

WELL, WE'RE PROUD OF YOU AND WE'RE NOT GOING TO HIDE IT. WE'RE ALWAYS HERE FOR YOU IF YOU NEED US.

OKAY! HAVE A GREAT DAY! AND REMEMBER:

WE LOVE YOU!

OOH, WE LOVE YOU, SWEETIE!

HAHAHEEHEEHOHO

SMOOCH SMOOCH SMOOCH!

I PAINTED ON A BRAND-NEW RACING STRIPE!

RACING STRIPE? HOW WILL THAT HELP?

EVERYONE KNOWS RACING STRIPES MAKE YOU GO FASTER.

RIIIGHT.

MARCH, CAN YOU HEAR ME?

YEP, LOUD AND CLEAR!

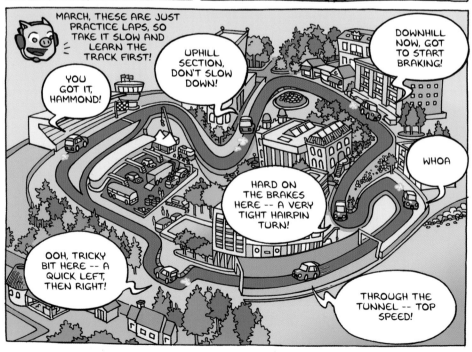

MARCH, THESE ARE JUST PRACTICE LAPS, SO TAKE IT SLOW AND LEARN THE TRACK FIRST!

YOU GOT IT, HAMMOND!

UPHILL SECTION, DON'T SLOW DOWN!

DOWNHILL NOW, GOT TO START BRAKING!

WHOA

HARD ON THE BRAKES HERE -- A VERY TIGHT HAIRPIN TURN!

OOH, TRICKY BIT HERE -- A QUICK LEFT, THEN RIGHT!

THROUGH THE TUNNEL -- TOP SPEED!

VRREEYOW

GOOD GRAVY! MARCH, YOU'VE JUST SET A RECORD TIME!

YOU HAVEN'T SEEN ANYTHING YET! I'M JUST WARMING UP!

WELL, REMEMBER --

THAT YOUR FRIEND OUT THERE?

ER... YES?

HAW! I'VE NEVER SEEN DRIVING LIKE THAT IN MY LIFE!

INCREDIBLE!

IT'S THAT RABBIT KID!

DO YOU THINK HE'S FASTER THAN LYCA THE FOX?

MS. FOX! MS. FOX! SOMEONE'S BROKEN YOUR LAP RECORD!

WHAT?

OUT OF MY WAY, BARKLEY.

VRRRMMMMMMMM

14

MARCH! BE CAREFUL! LYCA THE FOX IS JOINING YOU ON THE TRACK!

RELAX, HAMMOND! I'M JUST GOING TO HAVE A LITTLE BIT OF FUN.

ALL RIGHT, MS. FOX! LET'S SEE WHAT YOU CAN DO!

HAHA!

GRRR!

MARCH, SLOW DOWN! THESE ARE JUST PRACTICE LAPS, LET LYCA PASS!

VRRRRMMMMM

KRUNCH!

OH, I CAN'T BEAR TO WATCH!

MARCH, WHAT HAVE YOU DONE? I TOLD YOU TO SLOW DOWN! NOW WE'LL--

-- HEY! WHERE ARE YOU GOING?!

MS. FOX! MS. FOX!

AMAZING LAP

STARTING ON POLE POSITION

BEST CHAMPION

FASTEST TIME

PAF PAF PAF

YOU! YOU'RE NOTHING BUT A CHEATING BULLY! YOU DON'T DESERVE TO BE CHAMPION!

I DO WHAT IT TAKES TO WIN. I'M A FOX. FOXES WIN. AND DO YOU KNOW WHAT FOXES EAT FOR BREAKFAST?

RABBITS.

BUT LET'S SETTLE THIS ON THE TRACK. I'LL SEE YOU OUT THERE TOMORROW, LITTLE RABBIT. THAT IS, IF YOU CAN GET YOUR BUCKET OF BOLTS FIXED IN TIME.

WHIRRR
BOM BOM BOM
BRRRPPTT

OH DEAR
OH DEAR

MARCH, OUR BACON IS COOKED!

WE'VE GOT A BLOWN HEAD GASKET, THE TURBOCHARGER HOUSING IS CRACKED --

THERE'S NO WAY WE CAN FIX ALL THIS IN TIME FOR THE RACE TOMORROW!

WHAT ARE WE GOING TO DO? ALL THE WORK WE PUT IN TO ENTER THIS RACE! GONE! WASTED! POOF! WE'RE RUINED!

BOO HOO HOO!

THERE, THERE, SAUSAGE LINK. IT'LL BE ALL RIGHT. THIS IS TOTALLY MY FAULT! THE CAR WOULDN'T BE WRECKED IF I HAD LISTENED TO YOU! I'VE LET YOU DOWN, AND... AND...

PAT PAT PAT

BOO HOO HOO!

MAYBE WE CAN HELP.

...THAT IS, IF YOU DON'T MIND HELP FROM YOUR "UNCOOL" FAMILY.

HURRY, THE OTHER CARS ARE ALREADY ON THE TRACK! THE RACE IS ABOUT TO START!

PHEW! I THINK WE'RE READY!

HAMMOND, SHE'S NEVER LOOKED BETTER.

I HELPED WITH THE PAINTING!

YOU DID GOOD, JUNE-BUG.

Wing mirror from Mom & Dad's station wagon

June's good luck paw prints

Replacement quarter panel taken from Mom & Dad's station wagon

I JUST HOPE SHE'LL START...

CHK- GNA G

22

GNA-GNA-GNA GNA

COME ON
COME ON

BRR-VRRMMMM

THANK YOU SO MUCH, GUYS. WE COULDN'T HAVE DONE THIS WITHOUT YOU.

WE'RE ALWAYS HERE FOR YOU, SON. YOU KNOW THAT. AND MARCH?

YEAH, DAD?

REMEMBER, SOMETIMES IT'S NOT ALWAYS ABOUT BEING THE FASTEST TO WIN.

UH, OKAY DAD. THANKS, I THINK?

UNCLE HAMMOND, IS MARCH GOING TO WIN THE RACE?

I DON'T KNOW, JUNE. IT'S GOING TO BE TOUGH! MARCH IS STARTING IN LAST PLACE, BEHIND ALL THE OTHER CARS!

OOH, MARCH IS COMING UP ON THE FIRST CAR NOW! IT'S LEMIEUX THE CAT!

MROW! WHERE DID HE GO?

HE'S GOT HER.

YEAHHH! GO MARCH! GOGOGO!

CH-CHAK

THIS IS INCREDIBLE! MARCH IS PASSING ALL THE OTHER CARS!

MARCH, YOU'RE CLOSING IN ON CLARKSON! YOU CAN TAKE HIM IN THE NEXT TURN!

KRAK!

SCREE

MARCH, YOU'VE DONE IT!

THE ONLY ONE LEFT IN FRONT OF YOU NOW IS LYCA, SO BE CAREFUL!

YOU GOT IT, HAMMOND!

HI ♥

HEY!

PHEW!

HOW AM I GOING TO GET PAST HER? SHE'S BLOCKING TOO WELL!

BEEP BEEP

HAMMOND, I'M LOW ON FUEL. I NEED TO MAKE A PIT STOP!

WE'LL BE READY FOR YOU! AND MARCH --

-- IT LOOKS LIKE LYCA WILL BE COMING INTO THE PITS AS WELL.

HUP HUP HUP HUP HUP HUP

TUMP!

MOVE IT, YOU DOGS!

32

YOU'RE GOOD TO GO! *GO GO GO!*

HAHA! WE DID IT! *WE DID IT!* WE PASSED LYCA!

GRRR! WHAT'S TAKING YOU DOGS SO LONG?

SORRY MS. FOX! YOU'RE READY NOW MS. FOX!

GRRR!

JUST ONE LAP LEFT TO GO, MARCH! HANG IN THERE!

MARCH, GET OUT OF THERE!

SHE'S GOT ME PINNED TO THE WALL!

OH MY GOODNESS! MARCH OUT-BRAKED LYCA!

MARRCH!

PHEW!

HERE HE COMES!

YES!

I TOOK YOUR ADVICE. I SLOWED DOWN AT THE END THERE TO LET LYCA "PASS" ME.

HAHA, THAT'S MY BOY!

LITTLE RABBIT! THIS ISN'T OVER YET! YOU MAY HAVE WON ONE RACE, BUT I'LL BE BACK!

YOU HAVEN'T SEEN THE LAST OF LYCA THE FOX! DO YOU HEAR ME?

AHEM.

ALAN TUTTLE!!

THAT'S ME.

MARCH, AS THIS YEAR'S SPECIAL GUEST OF HAREWOOD SPEEDWAY, I AM PROUD TO PRESENT YOUR PRIZE FOR FIRST PLACE, THE GOLDEN CARROT!

I ALSO HAVE A PERSONAL QUESTION I'D LIKE TO ASK YOU -- HOW WOULD YOU LIKE TO COME DRIVE FOR ME AND MY NEW RACE TEAM?

FOR REAL? I- I MEAN, YES! I WOULD BE HONORED TO!

THAT WAS A FINE BIT OF DRIVING OUT THERE, KIDDO! YOU REMINDED ME OF MYSELF WHEN I WAS A YOUNG HATCHLING!

WINK!

BUT! WE'LL HAVE PLENTY OF TIME TO TALK TOMORROW. FOR NOW, JUST ENJOY YOUR VICTORY!

THANK YOU MR. TUTTLE, BUT THIS ISN'T *MY* VICTORY.

SKETCHES

1. Thumbnail roughs

2. Pencils

3. Inks & digital lettering

4. Final colors

Character design sketches

KEAN SOO

Kean Soo was born in the United Kingdom, grew up in various parts of Canada and Hong Kong, trained as an electrical engineer, and now draws comics for a living. A former assistant editor and contributor for the FLIGHT comics anthology, Kean also created the award-winning Jellaby series of graphic novels.

Kean's first car was a 1991 Volkswagen GTI 16V, which he drove and (very occasionally) raced for over 10 years.

Kean would also like to thank Judy Hansen, Donnie Lemke, Brann Garvey, Tony Cliff, Kazu Kibuishi, everyone in the FLIGHT crew, and Tory Woollcott for making March Grand Prix such a joy to work on.